Ferdinand Fox's First Summer

by Mary Holland

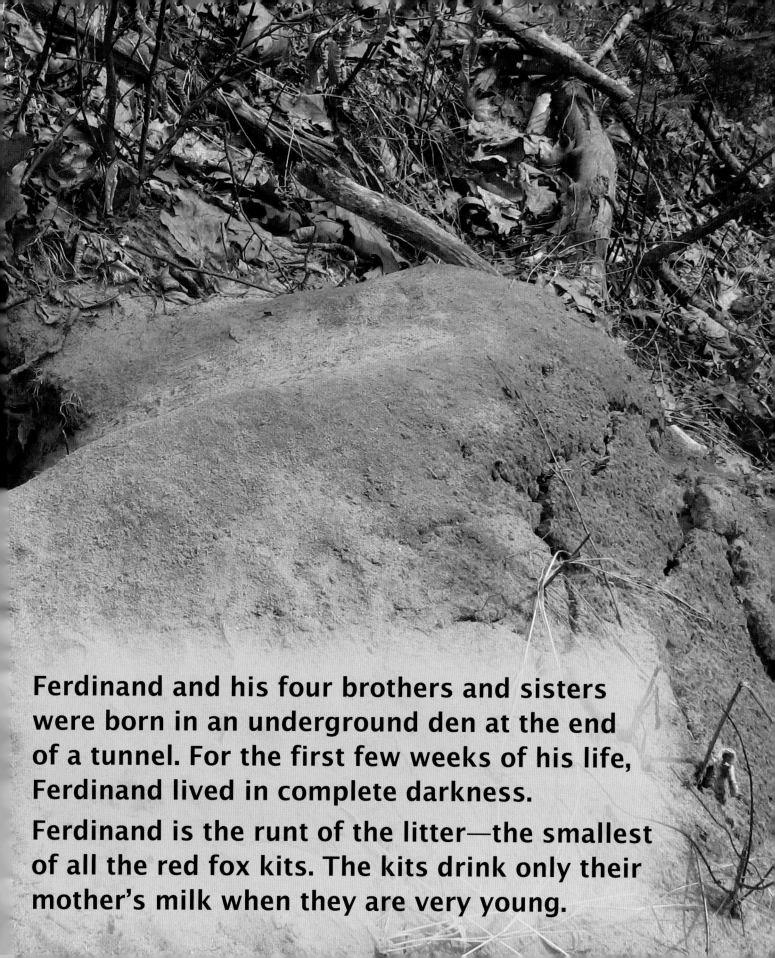

Ferdinand and his four brothers and sisters were born in an underground den at the end of a tunnel. For the first few weeks of his life, Ferdinand lived in complete darkness.

Ferdinand is the runt of the litter—the smallest of all the red fox kits. The kits drink only their mother's milk when they are very young.

When they are about five weeks old, the kits decide to see what the world looks like outside their den.

When they first come above ground, fox kits stay close to home.

The mother continues to care for and nurse the kits.
Ferdinand is the third in line today.

The mother also spends a lot of time grooming her kits. She uses her teeth to grab bugs and burrs from their fur and then spits them out on the ground.

Young foxes learn about the world by using their different senses.

Like human babies, red fox kits put all kinds of things in their mouths to see how they feel and taste.

Ferdinand picks up anything and everything he sees, even sticks.

Foxes use their ears to explore the world too. Ferdinand listens by pointing his ears towards the sound that he hears!

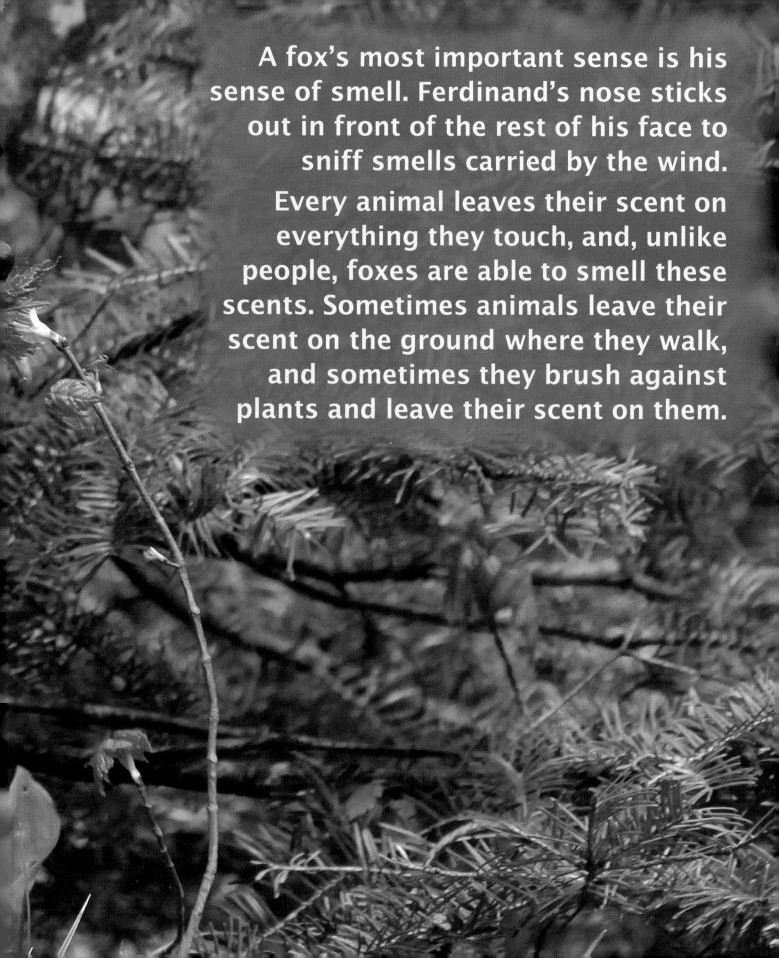

A fox's most important sense is his sense of smell. Ferdinand's nose sticks out in front of the rest of his face to sniff smells carried by the wind.

Every animal leaves their scent on everything they touch, and, unlike people, foxes are able to smell these scents. Sometimes animals leave their scent on the ground where they walk, and sometimes they brush against plants and leave their scent on them.

Sometimes the kits leap up into the air and pounce on one of their brothers or sisters. They are practicing for when they have to hunt for their food and pounce on a mouse.

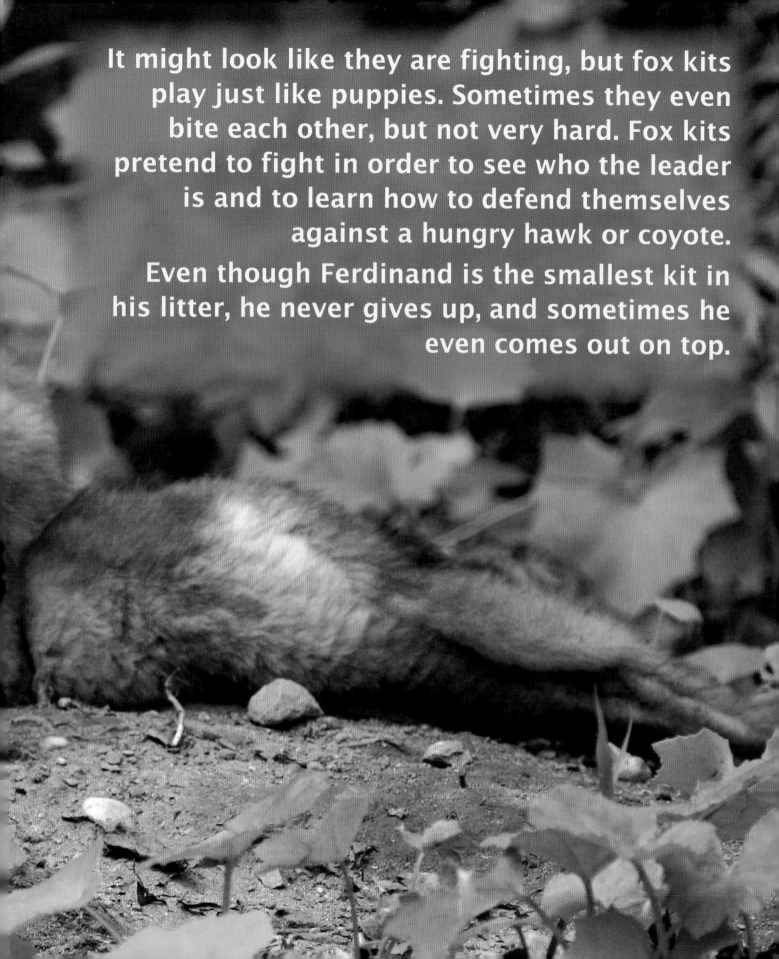

It might look like they are fighting, but fox kits play just like puppies. Sometimes they even bite each other, but not very hard. Fox kits pretend to fight in order to see who the leader is and to learn how to defend themselves against a hungry hawk or coyote.

Even though Ferdinand is the smallest kit in his litter, he never gives up, and sometimes he even comes out on top.

Just like human babies, as the kits get older, they start to eat solid food and drink milk. Both parents start bringing food back to their kits. The parents leave the den to hunt, and then come back and drop what they caught on the ground. The first kit to pick it up gets to eat it.

Ferdinand doesn't like the snake that his mother brought back, but he likes eating squirrels.

Soon, the mother stops letting the kits drink her milk. Sometimes the mother fox has to growl at the kits to stay away.

Without their mother's milk, the kits become very hungry. This makes them more interested in learning how to find their own food.

By the time summer ends, the young foxes get all their own food. Ferdinand is good at catching moles.

As the weather turns cold, Ferdinand and his siblings sleep outside on the ground and no longer use their den. In cold weather, they curl up in a ball and tuck their noses under their fluffy tails to keep warm—even in the winter.

Next spring there will be several new dens and new litters of foxes in the woods and fields. Ferdinand will be grown and busy raising young of his own.

For Creative Minds

Red Fox Fun Facts and Adaptations

Young foxes are called kits or pups. Adult female foxes are called vixens, and adult males are called dog foxes.

Foxes are related to pet dogs, but they are wild animals. Pet dogs, foxes, wolves, coyotes, and jackals are all part of the canine family (Canidae). Red foxes are the only North American canid species to have white-tipped tails.

Red foxes eat fruits, berries, grasses, insects, and other animals (prey). Their favorite prey includes mice, chipmunks, squirrels, voles, rabbits, beetles, and grasshoppers.

Red foxes are most active at dusk and dawn (crepuscular). In the summer, they are more active at night (nocturnal) because their prey, mice, are active then. Foxes may hunt during the day (diurnal) in the winter because it's harder to find food.

Red foxes stalk prey and then pounce to capture and kill. They can hear small underground animals and will sometimes dig to get them.

Kits learn to hunt by playing with their siblings. They practice stalking, pouncing, and even nipping or biting each other.

After capturing prey, foxes eat until they are no longer hungry. They'll hide (cache) leftovers in a few different places, often digging a hole to bury it. They'll return to dig it up and eat it a few hours or a few days later.

A fox marks prey it has partially eaten by going to the bathroom on or near it. This warns other animals to stay away from the food.

Adult foxes have huge, bushy tails that are longer than half their bodies.

Foxes use their tails to stay warm, to balance when running and pouncing, and to "talk" to each other. Like pet dogs, they wag their tails when happy and put their tails between their legs when scared.

Foxes rely on their sense of smell. Their noses stick out in front of the rest of their faces so they can easily smell scents carried by the wind. They use scents to track animals. They also use scents to mark and claim their territory and to communicate with each other.

Red foxes use their large, upright ears to find prey. They even point their ears to follow sounds.

Their eyes are set in the front of their heads so they can easily see and judge distances to pounce on prey.

Their teeth are sharp to capture and kill prey. Once they have killed their prey, they use their teeth to eat.

They also use their teeth to carry things in their mouths.

When the kits are about two months old, their blue eyes turn brown.

Can you tell which of these kits is older?

Red Fox Life Cycle Sequencing

Use the months of the year to put the red fox life cycle events in order.

By the end of **June and early July**, the kits have shed their fur a second time. Their third coat is usually bright red in color. By the time the kits are about 12 weeks (3 months) old, they are eating solid food and no longer nurse. Their parents begin teaching them how to hunt—usually one or two at a time.

By late **September or October**, the kits are fully-grown foxes. They leave the den area to find and claim their own territory where they'll likely live for the rest of their lives.

Kits are born in **March or April**. A vixen usually has a litter of five kits but can have as many as ten at a time! When born, red foxes have gray-colored fur, are blind and helpless. They drink milk from their mother and rarely leave the den.

By **August** the kits begin to go off with each other on hunting trips and then on their own. They still sleep together in the den.

The male and female foxes usually mate in **January or February**. The female (vixen) prepares her dens. She'll use one as the main den. Once the kits are born, the parents will move them to another den if there is danger.

Even though it is cold and there may be snow on the ground in **November and December**, foxes usually sleep outside curled up with their bushy tails wrapped around them to keep warm. Their fur is thick and warm. The dens are only used to raise young.

When the kits are four or five weeks old (usually in **May or early June**), they come out of the den. At first, the kits stay very close to the den. Their gray fur sheds (molts) and grows back in a sandy color to hide them (camouflage). The mother brings up eaten food out of her stomach (regurgitates) to feed the kits something other than her milk.

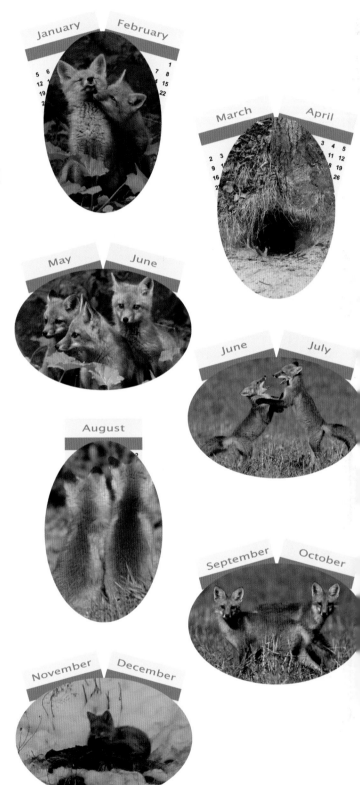

What Do Red Foxes Eat?

Which of the following things do foxes eat? Answers are upside down, below.

To Emma, who patiently sat for hours while I photographed Ferdinand and his family—MH

Thanks to Amy Yeakel, Education Program Director and Dave Erler, Senior Naturalist, at the Squam Lakes Natural Science Center; Helen Fey Fischel, Associate Director Education, Delaware Nature Society; Kathy Uhler, Director, Pocono Wildlife Rehabilitation and Education Center; and to Doug Jackson, Park Naturalist at Westmoor Park (CT) for verifying the accuracy of the information in this book.

Library of Congress Cataloging-in-Publication Data

Holland, Mary, 1946-
  Ferdinand Fox's first summer / by Mary Holland.
     pages ; cm
  Audience: 4-9.
  Audience: K to grade 3.
  ISBN 978-1-60718-614-4 (English hardcover) -- ISBN 978-1-60718-710-3 (Spanish hardcover) -- ISBN 978-1-60718-626-7 (English pbk.) -- ISBN 978-1-60718-638-0 (English ebook (downloadable)) -- ISBN 978-1-60718-650-2 (Spanish ebook (downloadable)) -- ISBN 978-1-60718-662-5 (interactive English/Spanish ebook (web-based)) 1. Foxes--Juvenile literature. I. Title.
  QL737.C22H645 2013
  599.775--dc23
                          2012030121

Ferdinand Fox's First Summer: Original Title in English
El primer verano del zorro Fernando: Spanish Title
Translated into Spanish by Rosalyna Toth

Lexile® Level: 930 Curriculum keywords: adaptations, life cycles, seasons (summer)

Manufactured in China, December, 2012
This product conforms to CPSIA 2008
First Printing

Sylvan Dell Publishing
Mt. Pleasant, SC 29464
SylvanDellPublishing.com